My Life as an Oak Tree

All in God's Plan

Charles Mills, Jr.

Illustrations by John Fraser

TEACH Services, Inc.
PUBLISHING

Copyright © 2014 Charles Mills, Jr.
Copyright © 2014 TEACH Services, Inc.
ISBN-13: 978-1-4796-0380-0 (Paperback)
ISBN-13: 978-1-4796-0381-7 (iBooks)
ISBN-13: 978-1-4796-0382-4 (Kindle Fire)
Library of Congress Control No: 2014921525

Hello, lady flowers and gentle trees! My name is Saw Dusty Carver, and this is Shirley Shall Crumble, my lifelong friend. We used to be mighty oak trees. Of course, before that, we were acorns! But I'm getting ahead of myself. Gather round and let me tell you our story...

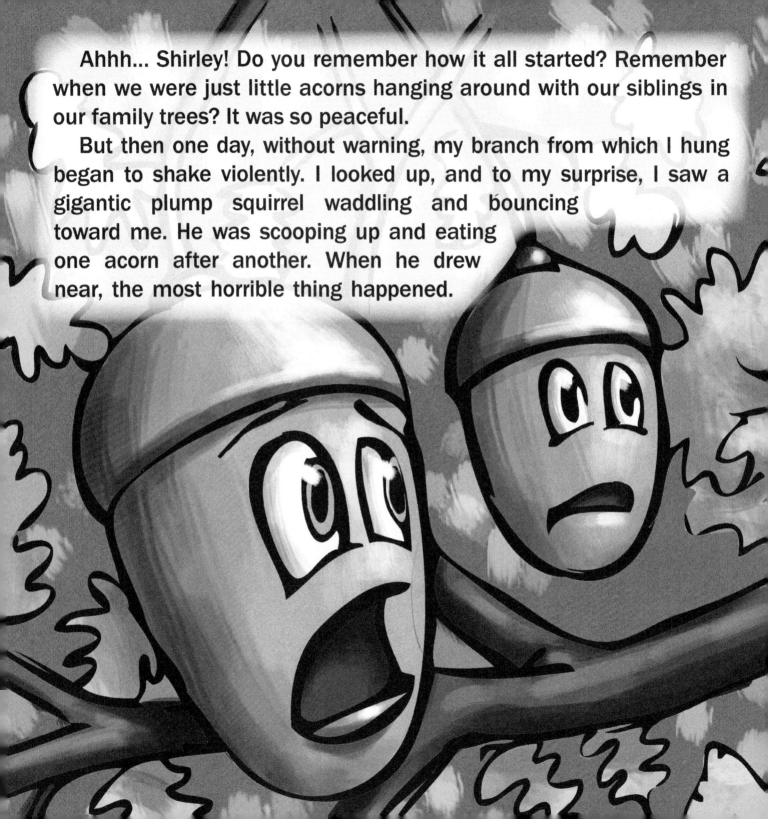

Ahhh... Shirley! Do you remember how it all started? Remember when we were just little acorns hanging around with our siblings in our family trees? It was so peaceful.

But then one day, without warning, my branch from which I hung began to shake violently. I looked up, and to my surprise, I saw a gigantic plump squirrel waddling and bouncing toward me. He was scooping up and eating one acorn after another. When he drew near, the most horrible thing happened.

The squirrel plucked ME from my branch—I was terrified! A greedy grin spread across the squirrel's cheeky face as he lugged a load of us acorns toward his home. Suddenly a blue jay squawked behind us. She was hungry for acorns, too! The startled squirrel lurched for safety with me and his hoard of acorns. Unfortunately for him, my branch made a sharp turn, but the frantic squirrel did not. Down, down, down I fell from the tree with a chattering, grumbling squirrel close behind me. It seemed as if we fell hundreds of feet before landing with a thud. That heavy squirrel slammed down on top of us, driving me into the soil. Groaning with pain and embarrassment, and forgetting his treasure, the glum squirrel slowly lumbered back to the tree.

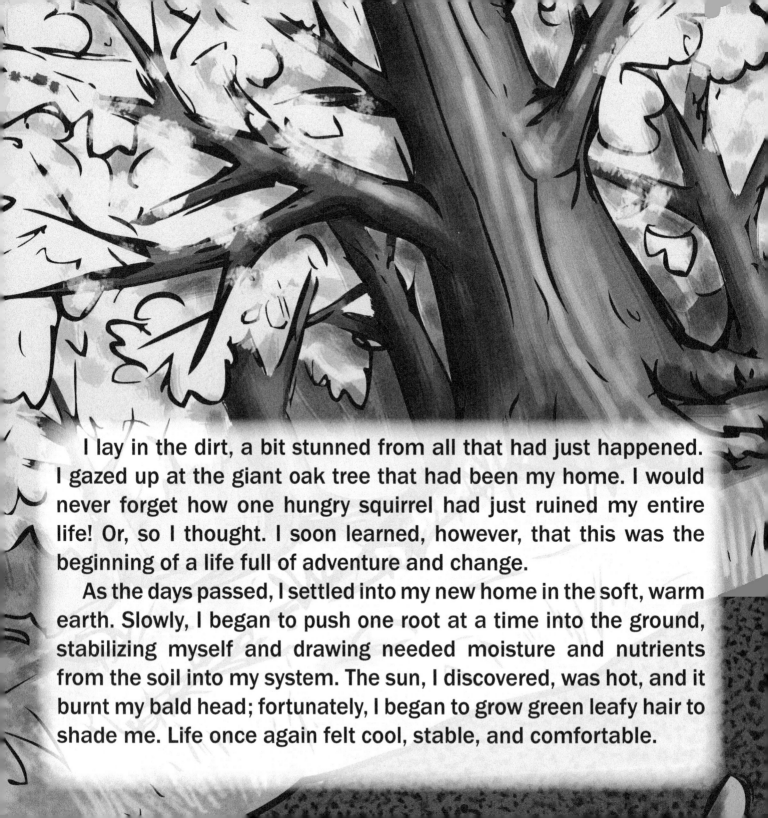

I lay in the dirt, a bit stunned from all that had just happened. I gazed up at the giant oak tree that had been my home. I would never forget how one hungry squirrel had just ruined my entire life! Or, so I thought. I soon learned, however, that this was the beginning of a life full of adventure and change.

As the days passed, I settled into my new home in the soft, warm earth. Slowly, I began to push one root at a time into the ground, stabilizing myself and drawing needed moisture and nutrients from the soil into my system. The sun, I discovered, was hot, and it burnt my bald head; fortunately, I began to grow green leafy hair to shade me. Life once again felt cool, stable, and comfortable.

But it didn't last long. Seemingly out of the blue, and to my dismay, I felt a pointy claw poke at me! I looked behind me and saw the hungry squirrel that had shortened my childhood tugging at my roots with his front paws as he struggled to dig me out of my earthen home. My green leafy hair began to wilt with worry as he bent beside me to scoop me into his cheek. But I refused to give up! I flexed my muscles and pushed my roots deeper into the moist soil.

Abruptly, a loud screech was heard and the shadow of a huge hawk passed overhead. Terrified, the frightened squirrel backed up quickly, tripped over a rock in his haste, and landed face down in the dirt. Spitting, sputtering, and blowing dirt from his nose and mouth, he scrambled away faster than I had ever seen him go. Fortunately for him, the hawk lost interest and moved on. Oh what a day!

Now, I wasn't always battling squirrels. There were good times, too. I still remember the day I met Shirley Shall Crumble, a cute little acorn that fell to the ground right beside me a month after I did. She was tiny, just as I was at her age. We soon became friends. I shaded her with my green leafy hair until she grew her own. Then I marveled when the weather grew cooler and her hair turned a pretty orange. However, when our hair fell off, we were both quite concerned, but happily, it all grew back the next spring.

Life was good as a young oak tree. God sent the rain and sun, and we grew taller and taller each year. Some of our favorite activities were watching birds and swaying in the breeze while the crickets chirped in the twilight. Shirley and I grew side by side, happy and contented.

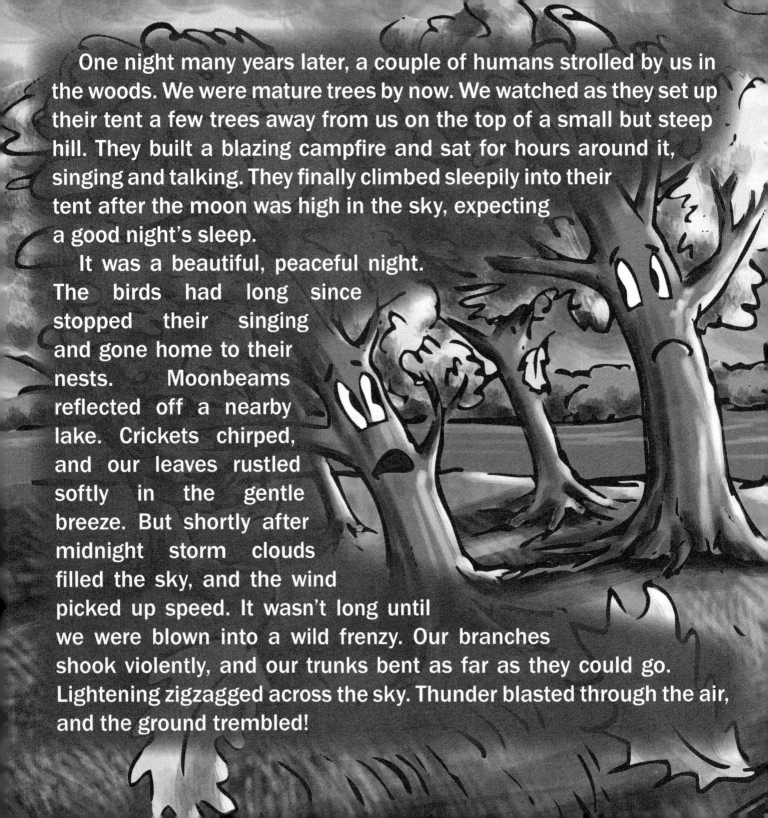

One night many years later, a couple of humans strolled by us in the woods. We were mature trees by now. We watched as they set up their tent a few trees away from us on the top of a small but steep hill. They built a blazing campfire and sat for hours around it, singing and talking. They finally climbed sleepily into their tent after the moon was high in the sky, expecting a good night's sleep.

It was a beautiful, peaceful night. The birds had long since stopped their singing and gone home to their nests. Moonbeams reflected off a nearby lake. Crickets chirped, and our leaves rustled softly in the gentle breeze. But shortly after midnight storm clouds filled the sky, and the wind picked up speed. It wasn't long until we were blown into a wild frenzy. Our branches shook violently, and our trunks bent as far as they could go. Lightening zigzagged across the sky. Thunder blasted through the air, and the ground trembled!

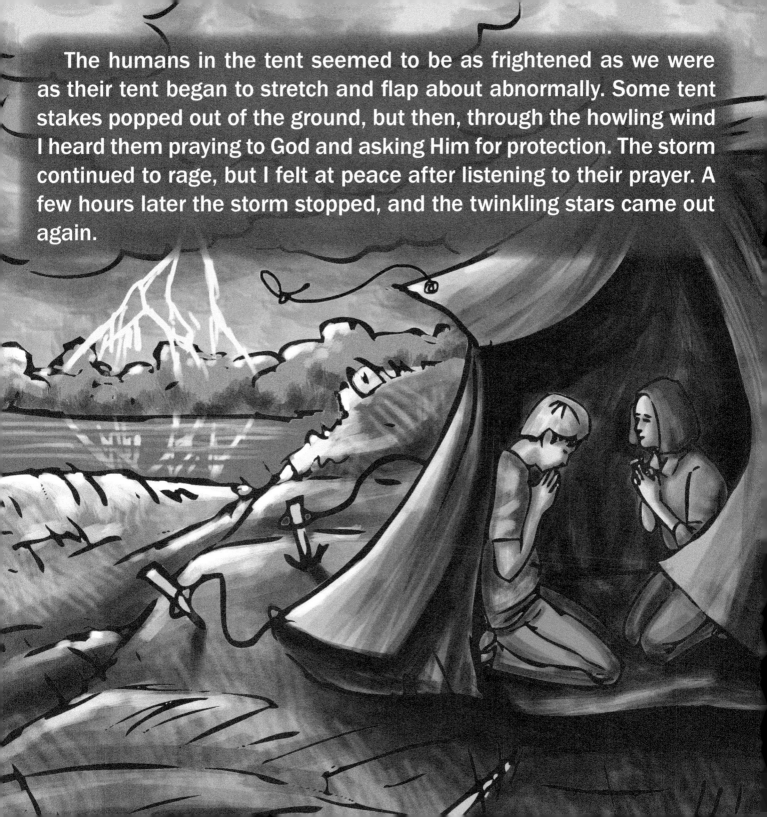

The humans in the tent seemed to be as frightened as we were as their tent began to stretch and flap about abnormally. Some tent stakes popped out of the ground, but then, through the howling wind I heard them praying to God and asking Him for protection. The storm continued to rage, but I felt at peace after listening to their prayer. A few hours later the storm stopped, and the twinkling stars came out again.

The years continued to come and go. Shirley and I grew taller and wider. As our leaves reached toward the sky, we began to see things we had not seen when we were small saplings. Sometimes humans rode on our lake in hollowed-out logs, striking the water with wide-ended sticks. Seemingly, the faster they struck the water, the faster they traveled. Then, when dusk drew near, we watched them jump and flap about as mosquitoes practiced skin-diving on their uncovered arms and legs. We also surveyed the nearby farm, which had more

animals than trees can count. Life was rarely dull for each season brought new activity to the forest and the surrounding area.

After many years, we were considered strong, stately oak trees. Shirley and I had accumulated many growth rings, along with a collection of critters living among our branches. It was good to feel useful. We were happy to share our branches with those around us. We thought we had found our niche in life, providing food, shade, and comfortable homes to those in need. We never thought that life would change. But then, once again, it did.

On a cool fall day, without any warning, some uninvited humans entered our woods. We watched as they cut down neighboring trees with a roaring, smoke-blowing creature, whose metal teeth spun in circles when the humans squeezed its' tail. Whenever it stopped, they fed it gasoline, and it snarled back to life! All of the noise and commotion made us nervous, but there was nothing we could do about it. And then, it happened; they cut us down. We thought our lives were ruined. We wondered what would become of us.

After cutting many trees on our hill down, the humans hauled us out of the woods with a gigantic green tractor. Then we were loaded onto the biggest truck I had ever seen. As we rolled down the road, the sweet smell of our forest home faded away, and the pungent odor of cut oak, cedar, and pine filled the air. Our truck drove up to an old building where tractors unloaded us into a huge bin by the side of a noisy building. From there we rolled one at a time into a machine. Long, wide belts screeched furiously as saw blades sliced all of us into strong, straight boards.

After being cut and sanded, we were sorted, bundled, and hauled to our new destination where Shirley and I were unloaded board by board onto a soft green lawn. Next, we were carefully made into a wooden frame. Eventually, we began to take the shape of a house—a quaint wooden house. It wasn't the same as our forest home, but I liked our new surroundings. Shirley also adjusted quickly to our new

way of life. When our home was completed, a loving family moved in and filled our rooms and halls with their prayers and songs of praise to God. It cheered our hearts to realize that we were a shelter, protecting these humans from the rain, snow, and sun.

Of course, our life here has not been without incidents. In our first year as a house, we were painted white with green trim. We liked the green trim because it reminded us of the leafy green hair we once had. Some of our later paint jobs weren't quite so nice. Shirley will never get over the year we were painted fiery red with soot-black trim by the owner while his wife was away on vacation. As you know, trees don't care much for the whole "soot and fire" idea— it reminds us of forest fires!

Luckily, this choice of colors didn't last long. The owner's wife had her husband sand us to remove all the paint; then he stained and varnished us to perfection. Now, our true beauty shows through for all to enjoy.

While I'm not sure what other experiences are in store for Shirley and me, we've learned to be happy wherever God has placed us. Yes siree, Shirley and I have lived lives full of adventure and change. From tiny acorns, to small saplings, to a majestic oak tree, to a quaint wooden house, we've discovered that whatever stage of life we're in, whether it's providing food for animals, shade for a friend, or shelter for

critters or humans, we all have a purpose in God's creation. Knowing this, we can happily and joyfully live through every new phase of our lives because we're a part of God's plan! Right, Shirley? Shirley?...
Zzzzzzzzzzzzz.

"For I know the plans I have for you," declares the Lord,
"plans to prosper you and not to harm you,
plans to give you hope and a future."
Jeremiah 29:11

We invite you to view the complete
selection of titles we publish at:

www.TEACHServices.com

Scan with your mobile
device to go directly
to our website.

Please write or e-mail us your praises, reactions, or
thoughts about this or any other book we publish at:

TEACH Services, Inc.
P U B L I S H I N G
www.TEACHServices.com ● (800) 367-1844

P.O. Box 954
Ringgold, GA 30736

info@TEACHServices.com

TEACH Services, Inc., titles may be purchased in bulk for
educational, business, fund-raising, or sales promotional use.
For information, please e-mail:

BulkSales@TEACHServices.com

Finally, if you are interested in seeing
your own book in print, please contact us at

publishing@TEACHServices.com

We would be happy to review your manuscript for free.

CPSIA information can be obtained at www.ICGtesting.com
Printed in the USA
LVOW05s0337100315

429913LV00001B/7/P